MUHAMMAD

MUHAMMAD

A NOVEL

DRISS CHRAÏBI

TRANSLATED BY NADIA BENABID

LYNNE
RIENNER
PUBLISHERS

BOULDER
LONDON

Lynne Rienner Publishers acknowledges with appreciation
the assistance provided by France's Ministry of Culture
in the preparation of the translation of this book.

Paperback edition published in the United States of America in 2008 by
Lynne Rienner Publishers, Inc.
1800 30th Street, Boulder, Colorado 80301
www.rienner.com

and in the United Kingdom by
Lynne Rienner Publishers, Inc.
3 Henrietta Street, Covent Garden, London WC2E 8LU

First hardcover edition published in 1998 by Lynne Rienner Publishers, Inc.

First published as *L'Homme du Livre,* © Balland, 1995.

ISBN 978-0-89410-895-2 (paperback : alk. paper)

Printed and bound in the United States of America

∞   The paper used in this publication meets the requirements
of the American National Standard for Permanence of
Paper for Printed Library Materials Z39.48-1992.

5 4 3 2 1

In remembrance of my father,
Hadj Fatmi Chraïbi

—Driss

TRANSLATOR'S NOTE

Driss Chraïbi occasionally refers to the cryptic and talismanic Arabic letters (*Ya, Sin, Lam, Alif,* and so forth) that introduce certain chapters of the Qur'an. The significance and function of these letters continue to be a topic of Qur'anic scholarship, but it is their presence in and of itself that is of greater import. They may be understood as the mysterious and sacred ciphers of a divine language.

—*N. B.*

This book is not a historical work, but a novel, a purely fictional account, albeit of a considerable historical figure, the Prophet Muhammad.

—*D. C.*

"Uterine ties augment life."

—*The Prophet Muhammad*

THE FIRST DAWN

*I*N A CAVE STANDS A MAN IN A SLEEVELESS, seamless mantle of undyed wool.

All the questions have been asked, their answers furnished; and now, in this the aftermath of human history, may the days of the imagination begin—the days of ascendant dreams and restoring doubt turned on headlong certainties.

Early in the seventh century, in a cave situated in the Mountain of Hira, just beyond the outer limits of Mecca, stands a man. He is of average height, even slight perhaps. Dark hair falls to his shoulders; his beard is dense and curly, and he is in the prime of life. He has light brown eyes, fair skin faintly burnished by the sun, a large finely drawn mouth, and front teeth set apart by a gap. His leather sandals are laced up to the knee.

Pens had been set aside and the ink had dried since astral times. And it was said that the Book's last word was written even before the first was given expression in any of the languages of humankind.

Soon the morning star will rise red and radiant. A man, forty or so, stands in a cave, a familiar cave, and begins to meditate, entering the absolute meditation that has become customary to him whenever he is able to come away and listen to the voice of silence—that peace the desert offers up most fully just before the day begins. Perhaps he also listens to his own peace.

Life had been good to him. He heads a happy home. Yes, two of his children, the boys, had died so young, but still, he had his daughters, four daughters and his wife, Khadija, who every morning and every evening and moon after moon enveloped him in tenderness, offering him the love of a woman and the friendship of a friend. He couldn't have asked for more than life had already granted him. He wanted nothing more. He had received everything a man could desire—he knew it for a fact. He also knew that he probably would not have more.

A tatter of breeze stirred up the branches of the olive tree that stood across from the cave's entrance, so green and alive in that wilderness of sand. It had yet to bear fruit, but its shade was bountiful. For years now he had retreated to this cave never bringing more than a small parcel of barley bread and olives. After eating, he buried the pits. In time, one had sprouted.

Pulling his mantle about him, the man listens to the ruffling breeze and smiles. He thinks of his sons; the children he buried standing up, feet first according to the custom of the tribe. Burst of my bones, marrow of my bones, most intimate breath of my heart, soul of my soul. Yes, and the earth that gave me day, the sun that gave me nourishment, the night stars toward which human dreams aspire, and the gallop of a horse mad

14

with gladness at the immensity of the desert and the blaring she-camel calling her young and the grain of sand, the chirping bird—all these had to mingle and stream through time so that one day a child could issue forth smiling.

The man in the cave smiles—slowly, sweetly. Is it not true that death always leaves behind it a magnified memory of life? Is it not then that bygone words and gestures become emotionally explicit, besetting us and clasping us to them: if one could only hear them, see them anew, pluck them out of the ground of memory, keep them from dulling and aging and reverting to oblivion—each and every one of them privileged. May nothing ever die!

From another continent a bird appeared, a rust-speckled, black and white lapwing lost in the night. Gliding on its back, it dropped out of the sky to perch on the mountain's peak. Had it gone mad to settle in the open desert, far from greenery and water, or had it flown skies so high that it had seen what mankind had yet to see? Incessantly flicking its crest, it let loose a long and quavering whistle.

The man heard the whistle and his heart foundered. Bird song always brought to mind the father he had never known. Wrenched by a question welling up from the depths of his childhood, he wondered why he regularly, and with increasing frequency of late, craved solitude?

Memories, far-reaching as well as negligible, always took him back to his orphaned childhood. His nurse, Halima the Bedouin, passes before his eyes. Looking back through time, he sees the words shaping on her lips, the syllables—the first, the milk syllables that she offered up along with her generous breast. He remembers his thirst, his blazing thirst.

"Muhammad!" she would laugh, "Catch your breath, ravenous child!"

In truth, she sang more than she spoke. In her unschooled and unguided Bedouin speech the letters of the alphabet took on a distinct dimension, outside that of the written or the spoken word. On her tongue, letters expressed their longing—yearned for the end of waiting, perhaps as when desire calls out to pleasure.

Ya Sin. The letters suddenly leapt out of the rock face. Scudding up his full height, from ankles to nape, they anchored themselves in his brain like sonorous bolts of light—*Ya Sin*—letters, clear-cut as stone, carnal . . . as though a swift rebellion had quickened life. Muhammad felt his soul surge upward and press against the oval birthmark at the cup of his collarbone. It was a moment of passage, at once fleet and slow, during which the image he had had of the world fell to pieces. When he came to, he was seated against the cave wall, a fold of his cloak pulled close over his head. It was as though he had just died. He closed his eyes and saw and heard.

Stars shone hot and glowing, flushed and fecund with female joy. They shuddered in unison, convulsed in unison—to the last, like birds of light caught by arrows in mid-flight. Overtaken by bliss, they gave up their souls without a sound. They fell with dizzying speed, not to the earth but upwards, far above the Milky Way.

Clouds emerged from the depths of time and banked themselves on the four horizons—panting, low, heavy and immaculately black on this torrid August dawn in the year 610 of the Christian era. A single sudden blast, just barely within earshot, spread throughout the expanse of the Arabian Peninsula. Then came lightning, a single bolt of lightning that split the heavens open in a birth of white fire that neither had nor would ever have beginning, duration, or end. It was born, it lived and died on the Mountains of Yemen, only to come to life again, to live and die again in the Hijaz and again on the Red Sea and there above Yathrib and above Mecca, in At Ta'if and in the Najd and further on and further still in the territories of the tribes: the Banu Mudar and the Banu Khat'am, the Banu Tay and the Banu Lakhm—and all the way to the enchanted gardens of Palestine.

Seven drums of stone fell out of the seven skies. Thundering as one, they shattered this here and now— this eternal present moment where the animal life of the human species holes up. Space grew, billowed by reverberations, by the throbbing tumult and its echoing afterclap that wheeled the air with the din of a thousand galloping horses. Like prehistoric giants single-handedly carting mountains before them, they advanced flanked by uproar and pandemonium, their voices rolling from every quarter. They stormed the gods, blew their kingdom to pieces. *Could it be that reduced to dust we will rise anew as life?* The wind, surging from nowhere and everywhere, circled the man meditating in his cave, immersed in the disordered successions that took him from reality to the dream where his conscience was laboring. Lightning. Thunder. Wind. The skies opened up and caved in, sweeping away the passing haven of beliefs. Materials that for centuries, generation after generation, had given them body and soul, custom and tradition and law, the clan, the tribe and the words of the tribe—were now all annihilated.

Unbroken vertical rains fell in blessed downfalls, in fluent and dazzling cascades. The sand hovered up to meet the water and guzzle it and fall back to the ground as coarse, green grass. The olive tree burgeoned for all to see, its branches suddenly as thick with olives as with leaves. And at the gateway to Mecca, out of the tombs dug side by side in the rock at the foot of the ochred walls, two child skeletons emerged, gathered up their skins, drew them on, and walked off singing toward their home.

The man named Muhammad didn't open his eyes. Pinching his index and middle fingers together, he pressed a pulsating vein on his neck. A shrill, whistling fear rushed into his chest true to the shadow of his most proud and noble core. He had an irrational conviction that something would happen before the day's end. He lifted his fists to his eyes and pressing them, he saw behind closed lids a vision of the long departed days of paradise, or was it a vision of days to come? Not the future that lurks in destiny, but the unforeseen moistening of stone and sand flats into humus, of a land entirely green, of fields of wheat and barley and spelt, and orchards, far and near—figs, oranges, olives, medlars, grapes in clusters and pomegranates—and trees, by the forest, aspen and sycamore, cedars and larch and holm oak, and a relay of valleys thickly carpeted in saffron yellow and reddish and azurite blues—luxuriant flowers; and a little farther off, grazing cows, heavy cinnabar patches in grass as green as the raw green of life in the meadows that stack the hillside, and humming streams and singing springs and music, the music water makes to set joy beating in the hearts of men and women, transforming them, freeing them from their fear of the sky and of the earth, releasing them from ancestral clans, from ties to tribe and race, from attachments to fortune and vocation . . . *When will the hour strike?*

Ya Sin. The man draped in his mantle filled his lungs with air. He shivered. He let the emotion rise within him, overcome him from the ground up. His thoughts came to a rude halt, and he felt the disappointment, the calm disappointment that steers visions: for as soon as he began to understand the true correspondences of the world, he also understood that all he possessed were the ready words, acquired since childhood, the Arabic words, old and bound to time and space—and everything he had felt had been beyond words.

He was awakened by silence, a rain of silence, a storm of silence. Somewhat halfheartedly and almost in slow motion, he lifted the cloth fold from his head, opened his eyes, and saw. Brandishing blinding swords of fire, the solar sphere rose with protracted rays. Outside, at a stone's throw (in reality or in dream) stood a stunted olive tree, gray with thirst. And far and wide, the hard earth baked by generation after generation of sunlight. Ever more bristly tufts of grass sprouted here and there like the scattered cast-offs of eternity in flight: woven into shields such grasses had once served to withstand javelins. As far as the eye could see there was sand and there were rocks, forsaken by the limits of time and space. The sky burned violet-blue, and not a slip of breeze to be had, not the shade of a shadow. In the dip between the hills, from the city hemmed by

19

palm trees, smoke that smelled of burnt cow-dung was already rising together with the morning hubbub of Meccans and the muffled bleating of their dromedaries. For a week now, these had been rounded up for a caravan that was to depart from the Northern Gate. Any moment now, they would disentangle their lanky legs and set off toward the Persian lands heavy-laden with dates and copper, brimming jars of herbs and spices, leather from the tanneries, Red Sea pearls and Yemeni silks. Everything was as it had been the night before, and on every morning before that.

The man named Muhammad drew up his legs and slowly raised himself. Slowly, he looked around him, questioning the ground on which he stood, attentive to the least corner of the cave—his cave—down to the smallest pebble. He observed his hands joined in a cup. Surely, these hands were his. He slowly passed the widespread fingers of his right hand over his face, his eyes, his hair, and the back of his aching neck. He was still shaking from head to toe. And then . . . The shaking stopped. Suddenly. Between his feet, he noticed a hole, a kind of small fissure faintly resembling two intertwined letters: *Ya Sin.* A metallic, sea-green scarab was making its leisurely way out of the hole. With utmost caution, it set off on its explorations. In transit, it abruptly swerved back on its track and chased rings around itself. It stopped as though to listen and fanned its wings, happy to be alive. All at once, blackness swooped in, death was on the path as a scorpion neared from nowhere. Hairy. Black. Its tail rose immediately, arched forward, and struck—the prey, clasped by pincers, was repeatedly soaked in thick jets of fluid. The chelicerae began their shredding motion, cutting into the scarab's abdomen first. The man named Muhammad raised his foot to crush the creature—then desisted from the act of destruction. Stepping over the scorpion, he left the cave. He felt empty. Empty and alone.

Fourteen centuries later, in the year 1993 of the Christian era, in a cave situated in a mountain in Azerbaijan, stands a very old man holding a rifle. Bewildered and revolted, he looks: in the cracked rock, a scorpion is meticulously mincing a small rodent. Devouring it. The man loads his weapon, one bullet would do the job, but something suddenly checks his impulse for human justice—*Ya Sin. Wal kitabi al-hakim*, ancient words from an ancient Book, a wavering memory, one he didn't even understand. Not then and not later. He left the cave, empty. Empty and alone.

21

*O*N THAT TWENTY-SIXTH MORNING OF THE month of Ramadan, Muhammad took the steep path slowly—a man of great outward calm and deep fragility within. Making his way downhill toward Mecca, he had the strange sensation that he was approaching both his birthplace and the first dawn when words were born. Every now and then he closed his eyes against the fiercely sharp sun and against his mind, so unreliable of late. But when he would open them again, willing them to neither blink nor stray, he still saw before him the dancing heap of jumbled sounds, scattering like the skirts of a mirage dispersing in space. He heard the sounds, but as one would an idea that has neither form nor pip, as a call to memory, a muted ringing, as syllables that were music above all.

He fought hard to preserve comforting reality. Desperately hard. *Ta Ha . . . Alif Lam Mim . . . Ya Sin.* The letters were inside him, grouped in twos, in threes, coursing through his veins, burrowing in the marrow of

his bones, at liberty to roam his body like a host of witnesses resuscitated from the dead. He felt that once, before he had lost them to the past, he must have known
them well, loved them so. Opaloid tatters of fog floated
by in the morning light; and also tatters of words that
joined and unfurled and blurred in the making, only to
rush back raw as life, every vowel and consonant calling out in its own voice: *"When the soul shall be asked
for what crime it has been killed . . ."*— *"By the fig and
by the olive . . ."*— *"Could it be that reduced to dust we
will rise anew as life?"*

And he ardently recalled the moment lived in-
tensely: the sweet and hoarse belling of the woman,
the beloved's face transfigured by love, so young and
younger by the day. Everything was confused in him,
rising in waves that churned in place, almost motionless, the flux and reflux of life churning as one, and
time was riding on the back of time. Reality and dream
were one and there was neither alpha nor omega.

Above him, a sparrow-hawk soared in the indigo
desert air. It didn't move a feather. Below him, a long
caravan glided through the flutes and clapping hands,
the pipes and drums of well-wishers. It uncoiled majes-
tically along the orange and violet length of the horizon,
and then it disappeared, taking with it the last camel and
the last note. Muhammad never saw its passing.

In a bend of the path, a skinny ash-white donkey
stood thrashing its sides. One of its ears drooped, the
other rose heavenward; its eyelashes were long and
black, and by its side, next to a scorched bush, stood
a man. He rested his head on the hands that were
folded on a stick that stood almost as tall as he. He
stood in the sun listening, listening to being. A white

24

beard grew to his knees; his skull shone bald and rosy; his bare feet seemed alive, crisscrossed by a thousand dark wrinkles. He appeared ageless—and maybe, thoughtless. Another bird of prey tore through the sky with a shrill whistle and joined its companion.

As Muhammad came within calling distance, the old man said:

"You are not possessed. Not possessed, no, and may the blessing of Jesus son of Mary be with you, my son!"

Muhammad stopped short as did the voices and visions that had tormented him from the moment he had entered the cave to meditate. Silent now, as though they had never existed. With a sigh he looked behind him to see to whom the old man had spoken. To a young Nazarene following behind him perhaps? In Mecca, there were Arabs who for years had kept faith with the Messiah. They lived in the eastern quarter of the city. Generation on generation of herders and artisans, who had always gotten along with the other tribes, linked as they all were by an ancestral pact of honor. Some of them, both men and women, lived as hermits in the desert, living off an ancient book whose silence almost matched theirs.

"You and I are the only ones here, except for my donkey. No one but us. Look at me, Muhammad son of Abdallah."

Muhammad looked. The bearded man was smiling, slowly, very slowly, patiently. In his mouth, dark nubs and bits of tooth moved about. And in the sweetest voice he asked:

"Do you recognize me?"

"No, not really."

"Ha!" He shook, first with jagged laughter that soon enough turned into a raging cough. Then he groaned a long while, trying to catch his breath. In time, he said:

"Ha! Well, I recognized you by your voice, your voice of gold. A golden bell that could have rung in a Church of the Kingdom. It's been thirty years now since I saw you for the first time, in Syria, in Busra, sitting in the shade of a tree. Remember now?"

"No," Muhammad said again, "not really."

"Your voice hasn't changed, and neither have you. Well, yes, you've aged . . . whiskers, a beard, your shoulders are wider, you married, you became rich and powerful. But big as you are, you're still humble, I see that. Humble and angelic, a child of forty."

Muhammad smiled his gossamer smile that creased his nose in the manner of a fox. He felt the dank trickle of fatigue and murky confusion on his skin; he felt heat surging through him, and he felt that at that very moment all the autumns of the world were being reduced to dust and all the springs were coming to life. He felt himself again, peaceful and appeased. At long last he had recovered his sight and found his voice. He said:

"Who are you? What people do you come from?"

"I come from the believers. My name is Bahira. I am a monk, a hermit. I've always been alone and I've never been alone, because I pray. But time is long, so I come and go. When time quickens, and men leave its path, I come and go. I left my retreat and came to help you."

"Help me?" Muhammad was surprised. "How, help me?"

"You were no taller than a dwarf palm when I saw you that first time in Syria. You were travelling with your uncle Abu Talib, may his soul rest in peace in God's heavenly paradise! He was in charge of the caravan. You sat in the shade of a tree, a cedar tree, and a small cloud had settled above your head. You played with pebbles and pine cones. Do you remember, child?"

Muhammad said nothing. He was waiting, listening.

"Isn't there an answer inside every question?" the old man continued. "Ask, keep asking questions of the questions. You're not possessed! You didn't dream. It did rain this night, a little before dawn."

For the space of a breath, there was white silence.

"What do you mean?" Muhammad asked.

"I mean what I'm saying," Bahira spoke gently. "Pouring rain, a storm to awaken the dead and the living, but as it didn't leave a trace, not a drop, not a vapor, no one saw or heard a thing. Except for us, you and me."

Pricking up his ears, the donkey made a small whining sound, but he stayed where he was, anchored to his hooves. Only his hide rippled in an intermittent puckering of bubbles and knots that began at the tail and ended at the nostrils. His master stroked him on the neck; quieting down at once, he stood stock-still.

Enunciating every syllable, Muhammad asked again, "Who are you?"

And not waiting for an answer, he stepped forward and stared in amazement at the old man's eyes. They were sweet, warm, absent. He put his hand out, almost touching them, and waggled his fingers. They stared back steady and unblinking.

"But . . . but you're blind!"

"Have I pretended otherwise, son?"

27

"You're blind yet you see? Who are you?"

"Bahira," said the monk. "Don't shout, I'm not deaf. May heaven grant that when the day comes when you are truly powerful, you will stay as you are, humble—humble and simple before your people. And that when the day comes when you will be called upon to speak certain words, no word shall resonate above the others. And may your actions never be guided by arrogance. Never forget the orphan you were at the outset."

"What are these legends? What is this sacrilege? What is your meaning?"

"I came from very far, from the depths of my solitude to tell you what I had to tell and not a word more. Ha!" and in a renewed flurry of coughing, Bahira got on his mount and went toward the radiant horizon. He could hear quite clearly that someone was calling him by name, imploring him to stay a little longer, but he never looked back. Not once. The donkey trotted off light as air to regain the familiar path where space and time converged.

At the mercy of his donkey, the old man made his calm way along the length of time. He was ageless— and maybe thoughtless. Thoughts were no more than shadows of the soul, and age to him had become a meaningless thing. As he completed his blind passage on that August day, he felt his past, his very distant past, leading the way with an angelshade and setting a pavilion of light afloat before him. On a day from amongst the days, somewhere on the earth, what is it that he could have possibly said or done to warrant his becoming the memory of the world? And who was he, really? He could barely say his name with certainty.

His name used to be Al-Khadir once, when he was with Moses, leader of the wandering Hebrews, at the crossing of the two seas. He had carried a rosary of fishes strung through the gills. Moses, deep in anguish, had wished to travel in his company for a few hours or a few days. "You won't have the patience, son," Al-Khadir had warned. A fisherman's boat ferried them across a river, and when they reached the shore, he had punctured its shell and rendered it useless, as a stunned Moses looked on. "I said you wouldn't have the patience." As they journeyed, they came upon a young man who was gentle and courteous and easy in his person; he had steered them toward the city. And in return for this good deed, he had been killed. "You cringe, Moses. You understand nothing. You don't have a speck of patience." As they entered the city, he silently demolished a standing wall. Three times, he acted gratuitously, dementedly—at least in the eyes of reason.

In the end, he said, "Our fates part here. I only left my retreat to carry out these acts you frown upon in your presence. That evening, a family of six was to borrow the boat and they would have all drowned; it was taking on water. The wall concealed a treasure sought out in vain by its rightful inheritors. As for the young man, had he lived a day longer, he would have killed his father and mother and his near and dear in a fit of madness. In this world, appearances can be so convincing as to be mistaken for reality, but behind appearances there may be meaning, meaning so deep that it cannot be seen. Listen to me. I may have augmented your torments by removing a few veils, but your mission lies therein."

29

And he shared a few words of advice with Moses before resuming on the path of time. And later, he did hear about a new civilization, but it no longer concerned him. In subsequent centuries it may have flourished or withered and weakened, but his part in it, his particular mission (or what passed as one) was finished. He lived between two eras of sidereal time, and the cataracts had already set their sight on his eyes and his name was Al-Khadir.

But before that, he had another name, what was it? When his peregrinations crossed paths with the triumphant armies of Two-Horned Alexander, what did they call him then? He hadn't said much to that one; in fact, he had said nothing; he certainly never warned him about Babylon, the city where his life as a conqueror would come to an end. An empire crumbled and another replaced it, and for how long?

When he entered Jerusalem shortly before Jesu son of Maryam, his name was Khidr. He never told that one either the way in which he would soon leave the world. More than any human being from among the human beings, Jesu son of Maryam was to embody the marriage of heaven and earth. Khidr had known it for a long time, but he had orders to hold his tongue. He only served creation; he was a simple intermediary instructed to speak such and such a word or make such and such a gesture in a given time and place. That, and nothing more.

The events that would overturn humanity, as in a quake, had all been announced by benign signs, small details as important as a nail paring or a wood shaving. He had always been attentive to those signs, had heard them clear as a voice. And for the most part, those events had occurred on a patch of the globe no bigger than a pocket handkerchief stretching from the Tigris to the Red Sea: a microcosm of the universe, a summary of history. He had never wondered why. Oh, no, no, no! It was not for him to ask questions, only to induce them in those whose path crossed his—in Muhammad, son of Abdallah, for example, from whom he had just taken leave. He was just a monk named Bahira, attentive where his brethren had been oblivious. He went homeward peacefully. He wished to rest, to listen to his bones. He was weary, so weary of life. And what could he possibly have said or done on a day from amongst the days and somewhere on this earth to have been denied eternal sleep forever?

*T*HE CELEBRATION WAS IN FULL SWING. Muhammad sat on the edge of the Zamzam Well and watched and listened. He thought about the monk, the old man met just outside the city walls who had spoken such sensible and senseless words. What had he said in truth? He wondered about the donkey; what terror had shown itself to alarm it so? And the well; why this blessed Zamzam singing away in the middle of the desert? Was it water then that gave life to all living things, to plants and people—even to language? Muhammad looked past himself and beyond his shadow.

In a blare of sounds and colors, people flocked to the Kaaba, filling the esplanade that stretched around the Temple. Some had come from as far off as Ukaz, from Ta'if and Badr; they had brought livestock and camelhair tents, provisions, and every last one of their kith and kin. Every article of clothing they owned was on their backs, capes layered on tunics despite the blazing sun. Kissing on the left shoulder in the Bedouin manner, they clasped one another and exchanged tidings of one and all. The name of this or that departed one missing from this year's festivities brought tears to their eyes. Then, suddenly joyous, booming with health and laughter, they would announce the arrival of an heir—most probably a son, vouched for by the ancestral science of seers. These too were in attendance with their divining tables and the shoulder blades of sheep that they would have to consult at length before offering even a stitch of advice, and with wands carved from horn that they tossed and twirled in the air. They would bend over these to decipher the geometry of their landings. The signs of destiny were many.

Red flared up in spots through the closely packed crowd. Cared for since dawn, the fires had been fed sticks by the armload, heaps of dung and smatterings of date pits in anticipation of the smooth round stones that were being tossed on then and there by all and some. In an hour or maybe two, when all the fire's heat will have slipped into the stones and when mouths will have rallied round to rid them of their ash, joints of meat sprinkled with pestle-crushed laurel root and black love-in-a-mist will be thrown smack on the stone to roast. Using a forked cypress twig, someone will pluck out the tiniest stones and thrust them still white hot into water jugs that will boil instantly.

With children standing all about, the older women—the mothers-in-law, grandmothers, and first wives—looked after the good things in life. Their experience equaled any man's, and they understood unspoken needs—the vigor that men mistook for valor. After a night of bungled virility, the men would often set out to hunt falcons or wage war against a rival tribe or simply to launch a routine raid. When they returned, all the experience, indulgence, and

34

perception of those they called the weaker sex met them at the door.

With their unbound breasts and carefully covered ankles wrapped from sight in strips of cloth that laced up to the calf, honey-flushed girls churned camel milk in urns that stood taller than their heads. Others, their legs planted firmly apart, kneaded rounds of dough that they tossed from palm to palm like jugglers. With shining eyes and half-opened mouths, they chewed musky gum Arabica. And when they laughed or chattered together, they all without exception—the nubile together with the pubescent—stole glances at the young men who pretended not to notice them. Many had come to Mecca to choose a husband.

Muhammad looked and listened, alone inside the familiar crowd. For things were what they were, and he was certain now that some thing was on its way, that what was meant to happen would happen to a living being before the night was out. He knew nothing of this thing, but it was fierce within him. *Matrix and maternal womb.* Some absolutely majestic thing. A tide of happiness and tears carried him back and forth between the shores of time. He resisted as he could, trying to shake his thoughts free—to come upon a clearing. But things were as they were, and some person whom he didn't yet know would soon, very soon, be overtaken in one fell swoop. Even then, Muhammad knew full well that something had lodged itself inside him, and every pang of heady fear that wrenched his stomach cut him to the quick. He took a deep breath of hot air and exhaled it. He didn't move a muscle. He stayed where he was, his expression serene as he sat by the Zamzam Well that for centuries had composed its water poem a few feet underground. He looked and listened, searching the eyes of those who stopped in passing for a word or a greeting. These people were his people. Each one of them a piece of the earth.

All around him, as far as the eye could see and the ear could hear, the air shimmered as poets clashed. Heralds stood at attention, hoisted on the saddles of their dromedaries in each of the four corners of the esplanade. They slowly lifted copper horns and blew them as one over heaven and earth. There was a vapor of silence, before the crowd rolled toward the Temple.

Platforms flanked either side of the Black Rock. Each dais was festooned by a canopy in which palm branches had been anchored. A sword of solid gold flashed its gem-studded grip on one of the tribunes and a horse swaggered on the other: exquisite prizes, bequeathed by the king of Yemen for the occasion, items that only the most noble of Arabs could hope to come by. Noble, that is, not by lineage or bravery in war or riches, but for possessing the consummate skill, the bounty considered priceless by all, of poetry. The king was a man of refined literary sensibility. He owned a beautiful castle and a flowering kingdom. But, for him, all the riches of the world put together amounted to little next to poetry. There lay magic, powerful and invisible as wind in the dunes, capable of transforming anything, every being and every thing. And Arabs, Bedouins and city dwellers alike, were as smitten as he was. It was the only history they had, and each tribe had sent its most accomplished poet.

Muhammad looked and listened. Between the platforms, a round and laughing woman held an incense burner at arm's length, rotating the smoke of myrrh and

36

frankincense that spilled from it to disperse the bad genies of art. To one side of her, a scribe had settled into a low squat, his knees tucked into his armpits. A wooden frame on which a rectangle of black silk had been stretched and a carefully sharpened quill soaking in a flint receptacle were ready by his side. By evening, he will have inscribed in his best hand and in letters of gold the poem deemed best and most beautiful by far by the majority of those in attendance. Afterward, the guardians of the Temple, tribesmen of Quraysh, would hang the masterpiece in a place of honor among the venerated idols. For an entire year it would be displayed for all to see, time enough for all people, Meccans as well as foreigners and pilgrims, to soak it in and commit it to memory. At year's end, a delegation of notables will carry it off with great pomp to the king of Yemen. He was a refined man—and a conqueror besides. Muhammad stood up.

He stood up and moved with measured steps toward the center of the square and the Kaaba. Bystanders turned as he approached and politely stepped aside to make way for him. He was Khadija's husband—and Khadija was known far and wide by all. And he was, above everything else, a Quraysh, from the clan of Hashem.

The golden sword sparkled away in the sun; the precious gems sparkled all the more, beautiful beyond a doubt and memorable to the expert eye. All the same, it attracted fewer eyes, drew milder praise and gasps of wonder than the horse. The horse was the thing. And to an Arab, horse was father and brother, mother and son, ancestor and friend. And what a living marvel was standing on that dais: its tail, pasterns, and ears were short; it was long in the belly, in the neck, in the flanks and the legs; its breast and haunches and forehead were wide. An immaculate union of fire and wind, its coat as impeccable as night.

Muhammad looked and listened. He smiled. Questions rushed at him from everywhere, fast and urgent. People sought his opinion: on the horse, on Yemen, on the distant lands he had visited. He had a fleeting desire to respond in kind, ask his own infinitely naked questions: could man outlive himself, and how? through poetry? but wasn't poetry like all art a merciless struggle against death—an enterprise in resurrection? Al Lat, peerless among goddesses; Al 'Uzza, goddess of power; Al-Manat, who snipped the thread of life: deities in a parade of deities that promenaded before his eyes inside the Temple, these were the gods of his childhood, they had always formed an integral part of his life. They were familiar spirits, familiar as the dome of the sky above and as the earth on which he stood. What essence of flesh and blood had the artists who fashioned them poured into them? and why? What sweat of their soul, what tears of their dreams had they breathed into them? What sweet hopes? dashed hopes? what reality? And after all that, had they survived? If not their deaths, at least their creations—even in their descendance, had they survived? If Muhammad kept quiet about all this, if he didn't bring forth an iota of thought, if a smile continued to float on his serene face, it was because he had no answer to give. "Ask questions of the questions," that's what Bahira, the monk, had told him that morning. And again the heralds blew their horns, four volcanic blasts of copper.

Amr and Qays approached, hailed by praise and cheers. Both were superior candidates—fearsome poets. They exchanged greetings, outdoing one another in mutual salutations; finally, they stopped and stood there face to face, ready to best one another with rhymes, stanzas and couplets. Thousands of feet stood up together, the crowd fell back, flowing out as a vast circle. And everything quieted down, noises and voices. There was only the panting sound of breath.

Joining his hands together, Amr started swaying back and forth. In a voice rich as bronze, he declaimed:

Desert Bride

> You and I, I saw us together,
> You and I, I heard us together,
> In the instant we combined.
> Your lips on mine
> Were water on fire,
> And I drank the opalescent fluid of life.
> Your eye opened wide as night
> And was entered by my day-bright gaze.
> And there, behind us, in the tracks
> Where the desert had joined us,
> Our feet came hobbled, stumbling
> On us, you and me, standing, embracing.

The applause was delirious; there was shouting. Muhammad looked and listened. He was like a man who had forgotten to sleep for a very long time. The fear had resumed in his chest, deep and sharp. He could make out Qays quite well, saw him taking a few steps to kiss and congratulate Amr, but he suddenly felt like a stranger in that crowd, cold in the thick of all that joy, as though he had just arrived in Mecca for the first time in his life. A woman's voice rose from deep in his loins and called him by name: "Muhammad!" Yes, home. He would go home, see Khadija's face again, that grave and sweet face again. Until his last breath, he would always remember how love at times could be lived and relived, a resurgent lull, a diminutive springtime of sidereal time. His body had not stirred and neither had his wife's. Not a gesture, not a word.

"Qays! Qays! Qays!" the syncopated call rose.

Qays unwound the length of red wool from his head and started to spin it in a frenetic windmill. Short-legged and fat, he was rumored to be a lusty, drunken pagan.

He said:

"After what I just heard, I am not sure I'll dare measure myself against so worthy a rival."

There were some laughs, some shouts. Then the voices rose mingling together:

"Go on, Qays! Don't put on so many airs. Every year it's the same thing . . . Go on, Qays! Qays! Qays!"

Qays closed his eyes and spoke:

The Year of the Elephant

A dream lights up my black nights.
Here, behind closed lids,
Sleep falls dragging its heavy curtain.
And the veil of former times lifts up
On the first poet of the earth
Reciting the first poem.

"O Hubal!" howled the crowd. "O Al-Manat! Long live! Long live!"

The fervent ovations went unnoticed by Qays. Transfixed, he continued loud and clear:

40

And, later, the successor questioned his predecessor
And the disciples questioned their masters,
In the languages of creation
That dispensed with words.
There was the tide of questions, and of answers,
Of books and of treatises.
If I speak like this, it is because I live
In a cruel and terrible century,
Disconcerting beyond expression,
When we must find again without delay
The source of the first poem.

A sprawling din, a burst of song and voices, drums and flutes. . .

"O Hubal! . . . O Al 'Uzza! O Al-Manat! Write, scribe! Write! Don't leave out a single word."

Muhammad held his breath. Qays seemed transfixed, only his lips were moving. He addressed the last verse to the four horizons:

Has a prophet been born among us?

Muhammad jumped, startled; a hand had landed on his back with the force of a bludgeon. Lifting his head, he turned to see a thin, bald, young giant of man studying him with commiseration.

"Umar."

"Still dreaming? You were at the cave again, weren't you? Are you unwell?"

"No," answered Muhammad, "not really. Could you take me to my house?"

NUBIAN IN A WHITE TUNIC RESTED against an ochre wall. He stood a head taller than his backrest. From far away he looked like a statue, plaster sheathed in anthracite. Umar yelled out to him, hooting like a town crier:

"So, some lounge about in the sunshine while their masters wallow away in caves?"

Pouncing like a man ousted from heavy sleep, the Nubian clasped Muhammad's hand and kissed it effusively.

"Master, master . . . Are you not well?"

Khadija had made a gift of him to me, when I had first started in her employ. On the day of my betrothal, I gave him back his freedom. He insisted on staying among us. He continues to insist. He claims it makes him happy. Can freedom sometimes seem as weighty as servitude?

On top of a plank that had been balanced across a barrel, a servant pelted away at the wash. Her arms were bared to the shoulder, and she had gathered up the folds of her dress and tied them in a knot behind her back. She stood in a rose-smelling spray of soap-wort bubbles, pelting and scrubbing. Close by, another servant was rinsing the front steps with vinegar water. The flight of six or so tall and wide steps dipped down a few feet below ground level. Muhammad stopped on the second-to-last step.

A water cask occupied a corner of the terrace. He lifted its outer cover and reached for the cup that bobbled on the cork lid that floated at water level. He filled it and drank to quench his thirst.

"What you need is food, real food," said Umar.

The water was of incomparable freshness; every day, morning and evening, it was drawn from the Zam-zam Well. He shook out the drops that had remained at the bottom of the cup onto his palms and brought his hands in a cleansing gesture, first to his face, then to his hair and forearms. He wanted to purify himself before entering to see his wife. And what waters were those, warm, subterranean, comforting, from which we surfaced one day bereft to life? The Nubian opened the double door with a majestic gesture.

"Enter, Master. The mistress awaits you, we all await you."

"And who awaits me?" Umar laughed. "I have a father, I do, and a mother, cousins, and so forth, not to mention a tribe, but who waits for me? I might as well be an orphan."

Muhammad stepped onto the last step. Gathering to him every morning that had dawned to find him still in the world, he entered the house.

When I crossed that door for the first time, I was twenty-four and I didn't have the least suspicion of what was about to happen to me.

He took a few steps across the terrace and stopped, lifting his head. Only a few rays of blazing light fell in intermittent shafts through an awning of palm branches plaited through bamboo, green foliage on a grid of yellow. Wholesome cool air filled the place. Umar called out in his enormous voice:

"I bring you back your dreamer of a husband. A little longer and he would have starved to death. Khadija, where are you daughter of Khuwailid?"

As if a signal had been sounded, shouting, laughing children bounded out of all the rooms that gave onto the terrace. The four daughters, their neighborhood friends in tow, threw themselves on Muhammad. The oldest had almost reached marriageable age. They all spoke at once, competing for first place: to kiss his hand, to nuzzle and be petted and rattle off every single thing that had happened that day. Pulling and dragging, they coaxed him into his preferred resting place, a divan banked against the wall.

Tapestries from Persia and Palestine hung in lieu of doors, shielding the inner rooms from view. The one from the Levant flew back cheerfully, and a tall, plump, graying woman entered. She had cut her hair; only last night it had fallen to her waist. Had she done it for him, to please him? Feminine. Maternal. She smiled, and the minute vertical lines that fluted her upper lip disappeared and the creases at her temples fanned out like twin deltas. Dimples burrowed mischievously deep in her cheeks. Her teeth were milk-white, her eyes petulant. Her joints were delicate, the ankles in particular boasted a hollow on either side of the tendon.

I dreamed her, I loved her. And, if tomorrow I were allotted the gift of writing, where are the words that

45

*could tell of that which has attached me to her for more
than fifteen years? And, even then, even if the sea were
full of ink instead of water, even those oceans of ink
would run short when it came to writing even the least
of her eyelashes.*

She stretched her arms toward him, and the flared
cut of her sleeves caught his eye first. Just as on the
first day. He had seen it as a gift.

"Muhammad!" the name came out of her in one
breath. "I was beginning to get worried . . . not too
much, but somewhat."

"You should have worried too much," blasted Umar.
"Look at the state he's in, hungry . . . and to tell the
truth, so am I."

*That afternoon I knocked at her door. She came to let
me in. She came, not one of her servants. She wore a
green silk dress fringed with gold. The yellow amber
bracelets that adorned her wrists made a clacking,
clicking sound as they appeared and disappeared into
her flared sleeve, and throughout that entire visit, she
had not once stopped moving her hands.*

*I followed her in. She showed me to a divan—I think
it may have been this one. She lowered herself onto a
cushion. She brought me a small dish of dates. I nibbled
one or two. She also gave me camel milk; I drank that
with pleasure; I was thirsty. A moment inserted itself
and its silence between us. I kept my eyes lowered and
admired the designs in a carpet so large it covered the
entire terrace. Never in my life had I seen a carpet
dance as that one did nor had I ever seen one as lyrical,
not even in the cities of Syria, where I had been more*

than once to accompany my uncle. There seemed to be a garden beneath my feet. Suddenly, crystalline notes came capering and tumbling out of nowhere.

I looked up, surprised. She was laughing, her throat unfolding. And the more I looked, the more and harder she laughed. I didn't say a word. I didn't do a thing. I waited. In the end, she calmed down.

"It's nothing," she said. "It's been a long time since I've laughed like that. Forgive me."

"Not at all, my lady."

She looked at me. Then she jerked her head with a small lively movement. A strand of hair fell onto her right temple and I was gripped by some powerful thing, impossible to define. I struggled to calm my breathing. With much kindness, she began asking questions about my lineage and situation in the world. She was already well-informed, knew what everyone in the city had known for a long time, but she wanted to hear it from me. So I told her the things I had been told about my birth and my childhood. My father died before my birth. I was entrusted to a wet nurse who, in keeping with the practice to make city children more robust, took me back with her into the desert.

She was poorer than my family, but she was very good to me. It was said that she loved me better than her own children, but I can't vouch for that. Like all newborns, my head was shaved and the hair weighed on a scale. Its weight in gold was distributed among the needy. I don't know if a little of that gold went to Halima, but word has it that I had a lot of hair—like now.

I paused. Why was I telling the story of my life to a person I had just now met for the first time and a woman into the bargain? She again moved her head and the strand of hair swung onto her other temple. Long black lashes gave her eyes a dreamy air. She said:

"I knew your father when I was young. He was handsome, the most handsome man in Mecca. You . . . did he leave you an inheritance?"

"Yes. A slave, five camels, and a few sheep."

"That's all?"

"That's a lot."

She took my hand, briefly covering it with hers. Very briefly.

"Forgive me, I didn't mean to offend you."

"Offend me? I don't understand, my lady."

I saw that again she was on the brink of laughter, but she managed to suppress it. She said:

"And afterward? You stayed with your mother?"

"Yes, until the age of six. She died in Yathrib, on a market day."

"What was her name?"

"Amina."

"Wahib's daughter?"

"I think so, yes."

"Do you remember her?"

"No."

I quickly revised that:

"Yes," and I explained, because I wasn't sure. "Yes and no. Vaguely."

"That's normal," she said, very serious now.

She spun a bracelet on her wrist, she seemed to be counting its amber beads. A very fine gold hoop shone in her left ear lobe, so fine that at first I mistook it for a golden hair that had somehow strayed into her black mane.

"Who took you in after your mother died?"

"Abd Al-Muttalib, my grandfather. He was past eighty at the time. We grew a great affection for one another. Then he left this world. I remember him very well."

"Yes?"

"Yes."

"And who took care of you afterward?"

"My guardian, my uncle Abd Al-Manaf."

"The one they call Abu-Talib? I know him."

"He is good and noble. But he has a large family and small means. The first time I accompanied him abroad I was no older than eight or nine. And later, he often took me along on his great journeys across the desert. He used to head caravans. He taught me the art of buying and selling. He also taught me endurance and patience."

Absentmindedly, she stretched an arm behind her to reach a brocade-covered cushion; she slipped it beneath her knee, crossing her leg over it. Then she said:

"You must be wondering why I have asked to speak to you."

"Yes."

"Do you know who I am?"

"Your name is Khadija, daughter of Khuwailid, and I am truly honored."

"Truly?"

"Truly, my lady."

She seemed to swallow something very quickly.

"What else do you know about me?"

"The things they say here and there—that you are one of the most important traders in the city."

"I am the richest tradeswoman in this land, to be precise. I didn't ask to be born wealthy, but that's how

things turned out. My father left me a fortune when he died. A large fortune. I married twice. I've been widowed twice. Both my husbands were men of some means. I didn't ask for that either. And now, alone and at forty, I oversee all of my concerns. And what do you say to that?"

"Yes, my lady."

She suddenly stood up; her eyes were all misty. I also rose. As she was taller, she leaned over and looked into my face; her eyes were black and soft. I had to close mine. She said:

"I am looking for a trustworthy man who can second me and manage my affairs. Are you such a man?"

"Yes, my lady, if you wish."

Her voice swelled like a stalled wind.

"The man I'm looking for must be the opposite of timid, he must look at what I say. You are no longer an orphan. Open your eyes."

I obeyed. Her smile was quick and vibrant.

"One of the caravans will soon leave for Syria; I shall put it in your charge. Are you ready?"

"At this very moment, if you wish it."

"Come tomorrow morning. By then, I will have given orders to my people. I'll expect you tomorrow at dawn."

I prepared to take my leave of her, when she caught me by the elbow:

"The journey is a long one. Three months, maybe four. Is there anyone waiting for you? Tell me."

What was that in her voice? Complete sadness? Mad hopefulness? I didn't understand. I was happy; she had just presented me with a means to earn my living. I answered:

"No, my lady. No one."

Her smile widened, blossomed.

"Ah, so, still not married at your age?"

"No, my lady."

"But, if it's not too indiscreet—you must have some-one in mind."

"No, not really. I asked to marry my cousin, but my uncle Abu Talib refused me."

"And why?"

"Because I'm too poor."

"Too poor!" Her laughter was uproarious, another gale. Except for her eyes, her face was all happiness. I waited a short while and then I thanked her for her hospitality and the goodness she had shown me. I believe that she may very well not have heard me; she was laughing so hard.

Lips parted, she kissed him on the forehead, the temples, the eyelids, the nose; she patted him on the back and ruffled his curls, unlaced his sandals.

"You're not ill, are you?"

"No, not really."

"You've caught a chill, the nights are frigid."

"Yes."

He looked at her, listening, barely answering. To remember and to believe: those were the keys to the long years of life together, to the uninterrupted present tense of their shared existence. Seen up close, Khadija's face had in it something of the nature of a book, a book with missing pages; the yet to be written ones. She too looked at him, attentive to the smallest shift in his expression. By his silence alone, he could bring such calm.

"Tell me, little father," the youngest girl asked, "you're not going to go again?"

"No. I don't know."

"Well!" Umar was in an especially festive mood. "Now that you have said everything there is to say, what if we moved on to important matters?"

His back was turned to them as he collapsed onto a pile of sheepskins, his endless legs stretched out before him like tree trunks.

"I am dangerously hungry," he added, "and from the tantalizing aroma filling the air, I suspect today's meal will be succulent. If you were to invite me to share it, to honor me with such an invitation, I think I may very well give you the pleasure of accepting. So? Are we agreed, Khadija, my good neighbor? Am I to stay? Thank you, I think I will. By all means. The pleasure is all mine."

Still keeping an eye to her husband's every gesture, quick and playful Khadija also let herself be drawn into the game:

"Who are you, stranger? And what occupies your days in the world?"

"I am Umar ibn al-Khattab, a day or two shy of twenty-six as we speak. I live very near here, in the second house on the second alley as you turn left. And I spend the better part of my time escorting sweet dreamers back home, dreamers so lost in reverie that they even forget to eat or drink. Satisfied?"

"No, not entirely. So, if I understand you, the spread is meager at your father's house?"

"No, of course not," his laughter was immense. "Quite the opposite, but I seem to remember your dishes as far tastier than ours."

They both laughed, matching one another in laughter. She finally collected herself enough to scold:

"How dare you come before me in that old coat full of holes?"

"But Madam, I too am a dreamer, but a dreamer who eats. Philosophy is philosophy and life is life."

With a clap of her hands, she brought the patio to life. A servant appeared, rolling a round table before her, another one followed to drape it with a cloth, and a choir of young girls bustled in to occupy a corner of the room. A first note sung by one of them was followed by a warbling of harmonizing voices. The Nubian pushed through the heavy flaps of the main door, his arms laden with steaming platters and stacked with flat breads that had baked buried in ash. An enormous water jug balanced on his head. He set everything out on the table and kneeled at Muhammad's side.

"Master."

"I am not hungry."

"Not hungry?" Umar, his mouth already full, could not conceal his amazement. "What a strange idea. Look at me, at my diligent mouth, just look how I eat and you are sure to want to do the same."

Muhammad didn't even glance his way. Surrounded by his daughters, he looked only at the Nubian. Dressed all in white, the black man at that moment suggested the succession of night and day, of nights and days. Carefully, he had picked up a round loaf and was indenting perpendicular lines into it, tracing on it with his thumb the places where it would be broken into four equal pieces. At that very moment, in a distant olive grove far in time and space, another man,

one who was life and death in one, took a loaf of
bread, broke it and shared it out among his compan-
ions. He was sad and good. Muhammad had never
seen him, not in reality or in dream. He said nothing,
thought nothing. A wave of nausea crested and ebbed
within him, bobbing like a pail in a well.

*When I came back from the trip, I went to see her. The
house was full of guests. I waited at the door. She bid
them farewell one at a time, with great dignity. When
they had all left, she took me by the hand into an inner
chamber where she sat me by her side. Partially turned
toward me, she studied me attentively. What was it in
her look? Complete expectation or complete absence? A
crystal lamp shone from its corner alcove. Olive oil
burned in it, encircling us both in a halo of peace.
Could that oil have come from olives that came from an
olive tree that came from neither the Orient nor the Occident, and could the luster of a lamp shed light on
light? I quickly looked down, startled to my being.*

*"No, no!" she protested. "You must have forgotten the
advice I gave you before you set out on your journey. I
want the man I deem trustworthy to trust himself. Tell
me, but look at me when you speak. And why on earth
are you shaking like that?"*

*I sat straight up, gave her a full account of my trav-
els. With many details I described the transactions carried out in Syria. I had disposed of the merchandise
with which she had supplied the caravan, driving a fair
bargain in a half a dozen cities. The purse from those
sales down to the last coin was then spent to purchase
goods that were sure to be rare, if not novel, in Mecca.*

"Things that will fetch their price twice over," I concluded.

"And I will pay you twice the salary I pay my steward and my warehouseman," she replied.

"It's too much, my lady."

"Too little, seeing what you are truly worth. Do you need anything else?"

What was that in her voice, all of a sudden so urgent and so raw? Her dress was simple. She wore neither jewels nor ornaments.

"What would you like from me? Ask."

Truly, I did not know the answer. Without the least transition, she said:

"I hear you arrived the day before yesterday. What have you done for two days? Were you resting with your family?"

"No. I was just outside the city, meditating in a cave on the Mountain of Hira."

"In a cave! You take such pleasure in loneliness?"

Again, I did not know the answer. I thanked her deeply, and in a dreamlike state, I left. I walked slowly until I reached the cave. Hasn't the lion ever felt weak as the aphis lion, and hasn't the blackest night been pierced by sudden light, and could a man who came from neither the Orient nor the Occident . . . Unclear forms appeared in my mind. I stretched out on the ground and fell asleep.

Muhammad looked and listened, serene among his own. One of his daughters was pressing his thumb in her tiny hand and another was stroking his beard with her face. The singers seated in a semicircle took up a qasïdah, an ode they called "The Beggar's Lament":

Thirsty, oh morning, I am thirsty,
When you rise and I rise with you.
Hungry, oh evening, I am hungry,
When you set and I settle into night.
I am love's beggar:
Such is my destiny.
Day after day, I spend my life
Seeking the eye
Of this one and that one.
Never a husband and not once a father,
I am the lover, that is my sad destiny . . .

The voices rose fresh as mountain streams, rolling off an infinite richness of rhythm and rhyme. Khadija laughed. A pigeon had landed on her hair to peck at the bread crumbs that she had sprinkled there for the game and the fun of it. Her laughter was a celebration with fifes and cymbals.

"You have not eaten," she said.

"I did, a little," he answered.

"Are you ill?"

"No, not really."

"Is it your soul?"

"I really don't know."

"What has happened to you?"

"I can no longer see myself, Khadija." He said simply that.

"Well," Umar intervened with his roar, "when the belly is empty so are the eyes. Naturally. When a plant isn't watered, it dries up like sand. When a camel shuns food for days on end, it gives in the knees and . . ."

His silence was instant. Muhammad stared at him in a stupor. Could the future be remembered? He saw this giant before him some years hence, skinny and bald in his old and mended coat receiving the surrender of the Emperor of Byzantium. From the depths of an ancient, very ancient fury, he shouted—through his clenched teeth he shouted without emitting a sound, inside himself he shouted:

"No! I am not a seer. I know it."

His face was petrified; he didn't move a muscle. Again, he shouted inside himself, louder, loud enough to break voice:

"No! I will not believe in these delusions. I am an Arab, any Arab from among the Arabs, a son of the desert with his feet firmly planted on the ground."

He stood up. Slight, fragile, and taut as a bow stretched to the breaking point. He upset the table as he rose. He didn't even notice. No one moved, no one spoke, no one dared. His breathing resumed, he heard it. He heard himself collecting piece by piece. He heard his blood slowing in his veins, and he heard the stillness overtaking the storm, and he felt the winds of doubt and unreason die off. And he went.

Straight for the door. No one tried to stop him. Rigid as a nightwalker, he walked. Peaceful despair swept him as he tried to bridle and exhaust and silence the source of his gigantic fury: for so many years, so much tenderness had surrounded him and kept him from the essential. The path toward himself was tenuous, so shadowed by joy and peace and opulence that his feet sank into every step he took.

At the door, he stopped and forcefully struck the water jug. It fell but did not break; toppled in this way, it resembled a pregnant woman. The spilled water rushed between Muhammad's feet, spreading the sound of birth. That was the first sign. Apparent, unmistakable. And because it was apparent, it could not be seen. *When mountains are razed, when oceans dry up, when stars will explode.* Who was the helper who somewhere, one day had stood by to assist the labor that would add life to life?

Around the time of my fourth trip on behalf of Khadija, daughter of Khuwailid, a woman came to my house looking for me. I vaguely knew her; she, in turn, seemed to know me very well. Her name was Noufaysa. She was a gay and lively woman, neither old nor young, and she said to me:

"Muhammad son of Abdallah, why aren't you married? I've wondered, everybody has wondered, all the neighbors. You're well past adolescence; twenty-five by my calculations and pleasant to look at; so, please enlighten me, if you can . . ."

"Marriage is not within my means, Noufaysa," I answered.

"Ah, so if you were granted the means, would you perchance entertain a union that promised beauty and nobility, patrimony and love? Would you?"

"What are you talking about? Who do you have in mind?"

"Khadija . . . pure and simple . . . the woman whose businesses you oversee . . ."

"You speak for her?"

"Yes, for her . . ."

"And how am I to hope for such a union?"

"By wishing it. Go ask her, ask her to marry you, she's expecting you. She's been expecting you for a long

*time, from the first day she saw you. To think that
you've been deaf and blind for all these . . . Go to her,
run."*

*That was a glorious morning. At sunset, I went to
pay a visit to my destiny. Khadija sat motionless in front
of the alcove where the crystal lamp perches. Her opu-
lent hair fell well past the small of her back. She sat
straight as an arrow, facing the wall; and without turning she asked in a measured voice:*

"Do you consent?"

"Yes," I said.

*A long moment inserted its silence between us. And
then, joy rose out of the heart of that silence: that laugh,
how beautiful it was, how true and inexplicable; it
echoed off the surfaces of the alcove, coming at me from
all directions. She didn't turn around, not even by the
breadth of a hair. Her voice was deep, deep and slow,
when she said:*

*"I love you. I love you because you occupy the center
of things, because when it comes to this or that you
don't favor some over others. And I love you for your
steadfastness and the beauty of your character and the
truthfulness of your words. I love you especially for
yourself. Go now. Go, I beg you."*

*Did she turn around, finally? and were her eyes
filled with that naked gaze that is the privilege of childhood?*

That was the first evening . . .

Fifteen years later, Muhammad watched the sun setting
behind the hill. He felt overwhelmed by his life as a
man—overwhelmed and weary. He had known real

happiness, a long immediacy, a continuum of chande-
liers lighting up today's day freed from pasts or futures.
So why the darkness now, forcing him to question
everything? What need have I for imperfections in my
luminous home? And when all is said and done, for
what, to reap what mirage? Could a single grain of sand
whip an entire desert of grains of sand into a tempest?
Could a vision, in all likelihood produced by fatigue,
defy my trove of peace and happiness? But doubt has
taken me captive. It persists, impossible to dislodge.
Day in, day out it has grown into certitude. And now: if
a single atom of that which has come into my heart
(the thing I cannot say I know for certain and that I do
not understand) were to be thrown on that hill, that hill
would melt. Yes, it would melt.

Muhammad looked at the setting sun. Life in the
very midst of death! At the end of the race, the sphere
of the day quenches its own thirst and floods the west-
ern horizon with the ruby thirst of humankind, and
with the emerald green of hope and the indigo blue of
reason and the saffron yellow of unreason. It immerses
itself into a sea awash in liquid reds, bloodying the sky
and the eye that beholds it. And there, at the pinnacle
of Mount Cham towering over the Gulf of Oman, from
the height of its thousand angelshades, the ball of fire
toppled in roaring flows. An hour or two along the
edge of time will find it rolling down mighty mountains held aloft by Atlas, the giant, braced on his
mighty calves, galloping through the valleys and the
plains of the West to plunge into an unknown ocean.
At that very moment or a century hence, in an ampli-
tude of human silence and ocean symphonies, a horseman shall slowly enter the sea so that his horse may

be lapped by chest-deep water. He holds a green flag slantwise across his saddle. He swings it free and plants its pole deep into the ocean. There is high water beneath him and emotions are high inside him; he accepts both tides as they rise. Can one language speak to all the world? Somewhere on earth, far and near in the sprawl of eternity, the membrane at the neck of a uterus uncorked bright red. The air was cooling, the sun setting, the noise of the town grew muffled.

Muhammad rubbed his eyes and stood up. He slowly started walking toward his home and the comfort of his family. Someone had picked up the water jug. Muhammad lifted its cover, filled the cup, and drank. And as he prepared to cross the threshold, he was overtaken by piercing fear; a rivulet of cold sweat ran down his spine. In front of him, before his eyes, he saw two shadows; his shadow was shivering, the second one didn't stir. He turned but saw no one behind him. That was the second sign.

He lay on his bed, resting his head on his wife's lap. Gratitude branched through his veins; immense quantities of gratitude fanned over him. Khadija stroked his hair; kissed his temples.

"Please speak to me."

He did not say to her: "When I was an orphan, you gave me refuge. When I was wandering, you pointed to the road. You found me poor and you made me wealthy." He said nothing of all that, but he felt it deep within him.

Instead, he said: "I was heedless this afternoon. The man who curbs his rage is a strong man; am I a weak man, Khadija?"

"Speak to me," she said again. "Unburden your torment. I am here, closer to you than your own skin."

"Am I mad?" He spoke with difficulty "Have demons possessed me? Have I fallen prey to a curse or a spell?"

"Speak to me. I know what has attached you to me and me to you for all these years. But I am older than you, sweet husband, fifteen years older than you. Why have you not taken a concubine, as I have asked you to so many times, a woman equal to you in youth? Or maybe a new wife or several as custom says men can. By now you would have had sons, living sons. That too is part of what torments you. Speak to me. Open up to me, I beg you. Empty your heart into my heart."

If he was aware that she was speaking, he did not hear a single word. Only echoes. He had strayed into a much more ancient time. *If you do not know what happened before your birth, you will remain forever a child.* Burst of bones and fleeting thoughts; slowly, painfully, he tried to gather up the disorder that had been fragmenting him since dawn. When he tried to put it into words, he came up with shreds of language, half-voiced in the half-lit room. The lamp at the foot of the bed gave sweet clarity. And Khadija's hand was sweet as it stroked his face, her lips were sweet and tender. He said:

"The woman who is here listening to me . . . is my wife. And Umar ibn al-Khattab is Umar ibn al-Khattab . . . and none other . . . and nothing more, not now or later . . . none other! I . . . am not a seer. No. Oh no. And the voices I hear are nothing . . . nothing more than fever and weariness."

"Calm yourself." Khadija was soothing, loving.

"Calm, calm, calm yourself."

"And . . . and there was only one shadow, Khadija . . . only one. I am witness to that. My vision is excellent, you know that. I can . . . I can count up to . . ."

And he grew silent. His Adam's apple pushed high up into his throat, and after a long while, it fell back in place.

"Go on," whispered Khadija. "I beg you, go on. Unburden your soul."

He couldn't have wished it more. The words were there, on the tip of his tongue, in rows, syllable after syllable—and he said this: "I can count up to twelve stars in the constellation of the Pleiades. But I no longer see myself, Khadija. What is happening to me, Khadija?"

And as he spoke those words, words in the language of his tribe, words that he could think and feel, other words instantaneously substituted themselves, irresistible words, whose meaning and origin he did not understand. Nor could he fathom their scope. And when they came from his mouth, neither he nor Khadija had ever heard the profound and vast voice that spoke them:

"And then Joseph said to his Father: Father, I saw eleven stars. And I saw the sun and the moon; I saw them prostrate themselves before me."

"Calm, calm, calm yourself."

With both hands, she reached for the lamp; holding it aloft, she brought it closer. She set it down without a sound. Muhammad was fast asleep.

N THE BRIEF BREATH BETWEEN DREAM and dream, in the stitch of a life or a death, the spent flame of the midnight sun gave way to the glimmer of nocturnal dawn. What harrowing passage into flesh was this? That night, dreams swarmed by fits, by snatches. Some streamed toward tangible forms, but most began and ended suspended in the air like tufted fleece. They called out to one another, echo to echo. The omega joined the alpha, swiftened by the centrifugal force of language. A language of image bursts. All, or almost all, the dreams were filtering one into the other. They were strung together by a thread, so frantic and so labyrinthine that it hindered consciousness and unconsciousness from meeting up with the essential dream.

Muhammad, deep in sleep, watched the birth of words. Dispersed consonants collected around the sky and the earth to merge into the Book, to bring it forth in a single birth pang without beginning or duration or end.

And all of humanity was no more than one of the words of the Book.

"Calm, calm, calm yourself!" Khadija kept saying, over and over again.

She was sitting at the feet of the sleeping man. Above her head, the silent, airy bats of incomprehension flew about in circles. Above Mecca, the starry sky was an abyss. In the neighborhoods, night watchmen came and went calling out: "All is calm, good people! Sleep, good people!" The heavy keys they carried rang in the air announcing their approach; their voices and footfalls would eventually follow.

"Calm yourself," Khadija whispered.

Muhammad changed the rhythm of his breathing and slipped into second sleep. Two gateways opened at once: one onto the edge of the sky and the other before my feet. I am going. I will go before you. I am your witness. What need have I for this world? This world and I, we are like the tree that offered brief shelter and the horseman who sought that shelter. Later the horseman leaves, leaving the tree behind. I will not return.

The Nubian whom I freed long ago walks by my side. His name is Bilal. I can see him head on. He is immense. A black rock has been placed on his shoulders. He climbs onto the roof of the Sanctuary. Stopping up his ears with his index fingers, he calls out to the four horizons. He calls out to me. But I can't hear a thing, not a sound. I give him sisymbrium leaves to soothe his voice. He chews them, but his voice still rises no higher than a whisper.

"Calm, calm, calm yourself!" said Khadija with extreme sweetness. "Rest. The fever will break soon."

A rope ladder tumbled out of the gate to the sky. On it, the giant Antaeus lowered himself down. He held up a black rock; but no, that rock I saw on Bilal's shoulders, that was Bilal's head, I recognize it. The giant stood on the last rung and reared up, filling all vertical space. He faltered; who made him falter? He fell; who made him fall? He died just as his feet reached the mother earth. It shook; the mother earth shook within us; it shook within me. His body spread over the entire expanse of the Arabian Peninsula. His blood emptied out into the sea. His backbone stretched from the Red Sea to the Blue Sea and crystallized into a wilderness of basaltic rock running through the heart of an ocean of sand. Palm trees rose out of his marrow.

Millennia of wind loosened pieces of basaltic rock. For centuries, dew collected on their olivinic crystals. Stampeding suns baked them again and again. Later on, sand storms carried them off as bewildered stars: some ascended to the sky, some remained on the ground, splendid as roses. A particular slab of rock outlasted inclement time and harsh seasons. It persisted—pure and black and cube-shaped. People came from all points of the earth to assemble around this rock. In silence, we stand elbow to elbow, we are ever so many, gathered on the esplanade of the Temple. A winged mare carries me away. Archers from my tribe take aim at me. Not one of their arrows finds its mark.

"Sweet husband," Khadija said, "I am here, close by. I love you."

Qays won the battle of poets. He rode a horse of flame and with both hands he lifted a sword of fire. Happy is the man for whom the poem and the absolute are one. Eliahou Ba Shimon, the rabbi from the southern quarter of the village, blew on the feathers of a white chicken; he slit its throat and sprinkled warm blood on

Qays's head. The crowd rejoiced, bellowed with its liquid voice. I do not hear it. I don't even hear myself. I am on my knees among the pebbles and the brambles. I move only by touch through the labyrinth of legs. I must find entrance to the passage, the underground passage that takes one to men from earlier times. They are calling for me from deep in their graves. *May our bones be assembled wherever they are scattered.* From Ur at the mouth of the Euphrates all the way to Bethlehem in Happy Palestine, by way of Zion, by way of Ararat, they are eager to entrust me with the meaning of their lives and of their deaths.

"It will pass, dear husband," said Khadija. With a crumpled handkerchief she wipes his forehead, his neck, his lids.

The question and the answer are engraved on a granite tablet.

"How am I to have a son when I already have a foot in the grave and my wife is barren?"

"It will be thus!"

At the foot of the mountain an entire people waits. They are seated in groups—by family, by clan. Their feet are aching and their tongues are parched. For days and weeks, after the sea opened up beneath their feet, they walked onward and forward across the desert without food or water. They have neither future nor present, only a past that weighs in each memory like a heavy stone. To trick their thirst they suck on flat stones. And to continue living they dream of hope.

The sun balls itself up, the mountain smolders. The Patriarch comes down the mountain. He has the sad face of a bull; now it is bent with anger. He throws the calf in a ravine. He smashes the tablet with his crook. Water springs up between his feet. In an earlier era, the guardian tribe, keepers of the Sanctuary and the Zamzam Well, had depleted the well and run off in the direction of the Yemen. Was this water the same as that water, sprung from the same spring?

"Calm yourself, Muhammad," Khadija said, "it is only a dream."

Muhammad moaned and smiled in his sleep. Once, when I was about five or six years old, Abu al-Muttalib, my grandfather, told me his dream. A shadow came to him and commanded him to unearth sweet clarity, the great kindness. "Unearth it, you will not regret. It shall be your wealth, left to you by your most illustrious ancestor. It will never dry up and it will forever quench the thirst of a multitude of pilgrims." He obeyed, and the Zamzam Well was tracked down anew.

Bilal walks toward me. He is joyous. Before him, at arm's length, he carries a black rock. The tribe of the Quraysh are assembled around us. I remove my mantle and Bilal sets the rock down on it. Each one of us holds onto an edge of the garment and we raise the rock to the height of a man. I fasten the cloth to a corner of the Temple. It was a moment of alliance. The Mother Book blew open and snapped shut. The hour had not yet come. I had to look further, to remember . . .

A boy is tied to an altar. His father prepares himself to perform the sacrifice. The boy's throat unfolds. The knife, sharpened on the spine of a rock, throws sparks as high as the sky. The cloudless sky darkens. Quails are falling as meteors in the form of birds. They are on fire. Khadija welcomed me. Without turning around, she said to me . . .

"I love you," said Khadija, "as I did from the first, if not more. May peace and peace and more peace be with you."

She blew out the lamp and lay down by her husband. She had resolved to stay awake. She fell asleep almost instantly; she was worried and happy. A smell of burnt oil and burning wick rose from the lamp, a slow spiral fading into the black night.

The scribe is installed before his table. He has come from the West of the West. His eyes are sunken and he is unshaven. Though the sun is bright, he feels cold. His eyes are weak and a film clouds his right pupil. Two lamps flank the table like witnesses. But he needs more light—a different light. He writes in characters of metal. He needs silence. He doesn't know where he is going; his identity is lost to him. It is like spilled water that runs but never strays far. He desperately tries to resuscitate me, to give his life meaning. He questions me with passion, with fervor and rigor in time and space. And what am I to tell him? He will be born thirteen centuries from now. Young children will enter the room and draw him into their games and sibling squabbles. He does not say a word to them, clenches his teeth. A cloud of smoke wafts around him. A river flows at the foot of his house.

Almost a billion human beings throughout the earth all ask me the same question: why are their children being killed? They tear one another to pieces and envy one another; they reach for the shadow and lose the prey. Numerous though they may be, they feel they form the lesser part of humanity. So, they withstand, they undergo. They call it fatalism. They keep a low profile, humiliated in their pride, ashamed of what they are and of what their ancestors were before them. Anguished, they ask me: are we ever to have a future that is other than our past? In truth, that is not for me to answer. Why don't they answer themselves? Their destiny was always in their hands, their earth did not lack for riches. Why haven't they destroyed the arms of destruction purchased at the cost of souls?

The dream flowed into the distant past—a large blue river bordered by sycamores and aspen and trees that bear bitter oranges. A wicker cradle passes by at the pace of water and dreams. Inside it sleeps a newborn child. He is swaddled in strips of cloth like a mummy. Downstream of the meandering delta, a woman beats clothing on a white rock. Each time she lifts the bundle to slap it down again on the stone, a rainbow drizzle of sun-irised droplets rains on her. She throws back her head and sings. Do you hear her singing?

> O River People on the two shores,
> The shore that was before
> And the shore that is now,
> Let the eternal Nile pass by,
> Let it pass in peace . . .

She has no children. Not yet. Her belly is a taut mound. Her husband is there, all the way upstream. Standing in his felucca, he hauls in a net where silver fish sparkle. Around the rocks, in the juniper, not one of the pink flamingoes is moving. And from shore to shore, and from sky to earth, legions of sea gulls fly. It is a clear morning. She sees the cradle and lets go of the wet bundle; holding her arms before her, she enters knee-deep into the water. Her breasts swell, harden, and her milk pearls into pearls of desire, of pleasure. Can you see the pearls?

The night watchmen of Mecca passed into the third hour of their shift. They came and went opening and closing the heavy doors that cloistered the neighborhoods. Their voices were muffled, reassuring.

"It is the third hour. All is calm, good people. The caravan from the Persian lands will soon arrive. The public ovens have just been lit. All is calm . . . calm . . ."

"Calm yourself!" repeats the sleeping Khadija.

In another place and another time. A very young girl retreats beneath a tree. She is filled with remorse, with pain and shame. An indigo scarf covers her braided hair. She weeps. Leaves murmur to her, the foliage traces comforting words all around her.

"How can I be expecting a child when no man has ever touched me? I have had no wicked ways."

"It shall be thus! You have been visited by our soul. You will give birth to a son. His fate will be great. Blessed be the day of his birth. And blessed be the day of his death. And blessed the day when he shall rise from among the dead."

Muhammad looked at the words. He struggled as they closed in on him, slowly usurping his old language. But he understood neither their meaning nor their intent. No, the hour had not yet come.

The young girl stands up and walks toward a cave, which she enters. A donkey and an ox make way for her. She strokes their necks and sits on the ground. She closes her eyes and meditates for nine months. The child that came forth from her belly is now in his thirtieth year. In an embalmed garden, he has been tied to a post. He smiles. He is at the summit of his greatest humanity.

"We have created life and death so as to make of you, yes, of you, Our finest creation."

They have shaved his face and his head. The hair is placed on a platter and weighed on a scale. Its weight in gold has been distributed to the thieves of Jerusalem. When he was thirsty, they gave him vinegar-water. The

72

branches exploded with buds; flowers flowered in profusion. It is the day of the Assembly, an afternoon bathed in light.

"Why, oh why have You entrusted me with this mission?"

It is a great cry that does not cry. The gate to the sky slammed shut, folding like black wings. There wasn't a glimmer in the darkness that fell on everything. Muhammad looked, distraught beyond expression. He desperately tried to wake up. But the hour had not yet come.

The man enters the city on a donkey. The post to which he will be fastened for centuries and centuries draggles behind him. He is sad, his sadness is absolute. No one stops as he passes, no one recognizes him. They had all loved him once, and he had loved them too. Muhammad watched as the sad man wandered by. He too was sad. But he did not understand. No, the hour had not yet come.

He turned on his side and sighed a deep sigh as if to oust miasmas of unreason from his lungs. The rhythm of his breathing changed, becoming peaceful and regular. His eyes rolled inward behind closed lids. Behind his retina all the shadows of that night of dreams mingled to form a single shadow that spun itself into a perfect circle.

I am sitting at the center of a circle of white-bearded men. I have been sitting for fifteen days. They are wise men, rabbis from Yathrib who have come to sit around me. They are the keepers of faith and science. Their faces are sober, attentive like cliffs are attentive. They have asked me about something I do not know, that no one, at least among those of Arabic memory, has knowledge of. They want to know who they were, those young ones who long ago, very long ago, left their people behind; and what had happened to them? For fifteen days, I waited without a language. Who was it then who showed me that which I was not yet meant to see and petrified my words?

Seven sleepers sleep in a cave. At the mouth of the cave, their dog also slumbers, his legs rigid before him. The sun when it rises moves off to the right of the cave; when time comes for it to set, it will have moved to the left. You would have thought them awake, but they have been plunged in sleep for three hundred years. And you would have fled, filled with terror.

I fled, filled with terror.

Someone hurtles me toward the future. Someone I do not know and I do not see. He leads me as he would a blind man. He doesn't speak—not yet: the hour has not yet come. By his presence alone he questions me. If the day were to come when I would return to my Arabia, my homeland, would I recognize its colors and sounds, its sky, its sand, the emotions that fed me like no other fire in the world? Friends coming from other lands, from countries that are not mine, visit me here, where I am now where time and space cross paths. Men and women, who have just now left life behind, come and kiss my hands and tell me that Mecca is very changed. Probably no more than I. Probably much less, if anything. Was it this, this disenchantment glimpsed in the distance, past their own existence, that made the Patriarch smash the tablets of stone and that made the man of the sad smile cry out his terrible cry on that Friday? Bursts of stones and bursts of screams can still be heard here and there. Yes, I am going to go. I will precede you. I shall expect you in the Garden of the Basin. I would like to enter the primordial waters of that Basin again. I emerged from it one day, but now I would like you to show me the way back. Take back my dream.

Muhammad turned onto his back. He held his hands together, fingers intertwined. Imperceptibly, the dreams were leaving him, their shadows and mirage fluctuations gradually receding. Underground conduits and countless radial paths throughout the earth would convey the fragments of unfinished dreams to others, men and women in times to come.

Armies began to move, altered by the Word; the music of the Word prepared the way before them. Until now, the sun had always risen in the east. Now it would also rise in the west as well as in the south and in the north. From dawn to dawn horses were galloping by the thousands. Have you ever heard the horses sing?

> Horseman and horse coming about as one.
> Throbbing and stamping to the same song.
> What death sets off their dash for life?
> What life their dash for death, at every turn?
> Streaming banners snap.
> Drawn blades sparkle.
> The fine luster of naked souls is everywhere.

Mountains and droughts. Valleys and plains. Rivers, seas, and open skies that sometimes pour with heavy rains. Blessed rains. Rains to cleanse bodies, to wash thoughts free of grime, to wash tomorrow's blue. Stomping hooves stomp continuously. Light spurts in sprays from pooling waters and pebbles are reduced to dust. The dust of the earth floats upward and mixes with the dust of stars. The wind seethes at a passing multitude. Grass thickens and new grass is born. Secular, sumptuous, powerful empires fall, others rise in their stead. Men on horses squint at the horizon, quickly leafing past mirages. The horizon retreats into infinity. Beyond the horizon lurks the dream, clear and concrete, before it too retreats. Here and there on the planet, a few have steadied the dream and secured it to time. Most others are still pursuing it. Out of their deserts and leaving their emptied selves behind, kings have moored themselves in the emptiness of power. The Arts flourish, the tree of Science flowers.

"The caravan from Persia has arrived," the night watchmen announce in muffled voices. "All is calm, good people. The sun will not be long now."

The man chews it by small mouthfuls. This griddle bread kneaded with olive oil will be most of his daily fare. But he is not a hungry man in the usual sense. Instead, he hungers for being, for things that lie beyond art and science; he thirsts after the unfathomable. His name is Muhyi'ldin Ibn Arabi. He is a thin man, average in height and dressed as plainly as a monk. The top of his head is balding; his eyelids are fragile as wafers; his black brows are coarse and bushy; he is beardless. Ink stains extend like feelers, lining the grooves of the palm, back, and especially the fingertips of his right hand. The quill stands in the inkwell. The well is dry. Ibn Arabi has just used up the last drops to write the last words of *The Gems of Knowledge*. Over the years, he has written many books, but this is his last, his newborn. He is still shuddering from the effort, and the sleeper shudders with him. Who, who weeps—weeps without a sound? Are tears pearls of the mind, like dew collecting in the blackest night? Are they the best a feeling, thinking man may offer? Ibn Arabi feels empty, empty and alone. He never rereads his work; a woman who has just given birth cannot give the same birth twice. Posterity will take care of that for him—perhaps. He wants neither reward nor reassurance. For who can look beyond his own gaze?

An empty room. It is here that he has kept vigil and reflected with the eyes of the mind. In this room he conceived, doubted, and emerged from doubt only to permanently install his doubt in long-held certitudes. How can the true correspondences of the world be displayed: vision, form, images, signs, imagination? A small room with its whitewashed walls. Monastical. A cow's hide serves for a bed and a tree limb for a pillow. A bit of candle burns and smokes. Just past Ibn Arabi's door, Andalusia glitters with a thousand flares. He has not retreated from the world; the world retreated from him in its opulence and magnificence. In his sleep, Muhammad looked.

Centuries and civilizations later, another man withdrew from the world. A sixty-year-old man named Daniel. He is reserved, straight as an arrow even when he sits. His beard is thin and his eyes are honest and full of kindness. He is rereading *The Gems of Knowledge*. And as always, the book transports his mind and his eyes: superb, shimmering words unearthed from the heart of language. For whom were these gems of language destined? On a Friday in spring, Daniel sits surrounded by his very large family in a garden of linden trees and holm oaks. He listens to all, knows the right word for each one. A fleet yet lasting sensation passes over him: is he being summoned to another family gathering? Has one of those imaginary presences that in another time summoned Ibn Arabi come for him? Past the door of this home, the spirit of matter reigns in all its plenitude. Muhammad looked.

In sad Palestine, children pick up the splinters of a broken tablet and hurl them at the descendant of the Patriarch. The earth drinks the blood. A gigantic axe splits the land, cutting clean through the plateau. Shattered basaltic rock spouts jets of black and oily water. The descendants of the guardians of the Temple purify themselves in it, guzzle it down. Nearer to the sleeper, under his bed, an African woman rocks her husband and gives him her frail breast. Her newborn child died of hunger.

"Awaken!"

All at once all the dreams streamed down in a dazzling cascade. Toward the end of the night, consciousness on the point of emergence drew back into unconsciousness like a riptide with its fringe of foam. A rising tide caught up to them and spun them in its dizzy pit: the emptiness of the real and the being of the unreal.

"You, wrapped in your mantle, awaken!"

Muhammad watched the dreams flee into what little sleep was left. He could see their outlines clearly as they faded away. But he could not see why he had dreamt all he had dreamt since the sun had set.

"Awaken!"

He struggled, his will pulled taut as a stretched bow; to the marrow of his bones he struggled. He desperately resisted the forceful breath that pulled him toward awakening.

"Awaken! The hour has come."

Someone shook him firmly by the shoulder. He awakened and so did all his senses.

That night when I woke up, I was no longer the same man. Khadija was sleeping peacefully. There was no one else in the room.

THE SECOND DAWN

*Q*AYS HAD NOT CEASED MARVELLING SINCE the previous evening. He had escorted this prince of thoroughbreds, his poet's prize won in competition, toward his house, the folds of his coat clearing a path for the horse to step into.

"Come in, friend, come!" he whispered to the horse. "This is your home and I am your servant."

In the doorway, tears ran down his face—tears of goodness, of pure-heartedness, of joy. And of pride. So poetry did make sense! It could widen horizons and broaden hearts, even the heart of the powerful king of Yemen. He put the horse in the best room—the one reserved to honor passing strangers—and resting his head on the great neck, he slept fast by the animal and dreamt of fire, azure blues, and wind. Until . . . later, an hour before sunrise, when he woke up with a start.

Night watchmen were unbolting the neighborhood gates one by one and gathering on the esplanade adjoining the Sanctuary. One of them brought the viaticum, flat breads, and a necklace of fried dough rings strung on a palm leaf. Standing, they partook of the food fairly and exchanged the scant news that collects in the night and congratulated one another on being good watchmen. At their feet, flames danced in the brazier. Soon now they would return to their houses and their sleep-warmed wives. Suddenly, they saw a man preceded by a horse coming toward them. Recognizing him they called to him: "Qays! Ho! Qays!" Granting them neither word nor glance, Qays walked straight to the Temple, unhooked the square of silk on which the scribe had set down his poem in golden letters, tore it and slashed it and threw it in the rivulet of sullied waters and then went into the night. The horse's hooves sounded for a long time in the silence that had fallen as sudden as a stone.

It was the twenty-seventh night of Ramadan, roundabout mid-August of the year 610 of the Christian calendar. A man, forty or so, dressed in a sleeveless, seamless mantle of undyed wool, advanced toward his destiny. Premonitions had not alerted him to that destiny, not yet. There had been only this, an unspeakable urgency that had driven him bareheaded and barefoot from his bed and sent him coursing inevitably toward the Mountain of Hira. In the innermost recesses of that part of him that was most proud and most noble, he believed that all the moments of his existence, the most remote as well as the most immediate, the most solemn as well as the most futile, now accompanied him step by step. A shade, blacker than darkness, preceded him and clearly pointed the way. Two or three times he stopped and surveyed the surrounding darkness. He was alone, not even the hair of a shadow fell from his body. The shadow was there, before him, also stopping, impatient and menacing.

"The hour draws near."

And again he walked. The star-seeded sky above him convulsed in long and continuous, almost seismic shivers. The man was now shaking from head to toe. For an instant, he thought of turning back, back to his home and his past. He wanted that. Only that. For a very brief and celestial moment, his will and wish stretched to the breaking point. And he felt himself hurtling toward the future.

"The hour draws near."

And was it foretold that on that night the keenest sense would reside in the ear, not the eye? Was it possible that images, unsaid, voiceless images, would ring in the ear first? And were eyes no more than thinking stones? Had Mecca broken its bounds and cleared the valley to spread over all creation? As he walked, the man beheld a city disclosed in its cadences. On one of its outlying hills a rooster, throat puffed, readied himself to crow. On hills and terraces, far and near, others stood at attention facing the eastern sky and prepared to retort. One of them, the oldest one, dropped, just like that, off the wall where he had slept since dusk the night before. Stiff-winged, his lids half-opened, half-closed, and pink, he shuddered his last shudder.

A horse tugged on his tether, producing an occasional metallic clanging. A fenced-in mare exhaled through her nostrils, whimpering softly behind the paling. And crickets high and low twanged their elytra. Palm trees bent from great heights to whisper news of the coming day to the sleep-filled earth.

"The hour draws near."

Tree bark crackled. Slabs of rock that stacked the hill-side also crackled. In the patios, breads were rising between the warm cloth and the wooden board. Yeast bubbles popped one at a time.

Deep in the bedrock, in Mecca's underbelly, water burbled to form the water table that fed the Zamzam Well. Each drop was the first and the ultimate. On level ground, somewhere off to the side, a pair of caddis-flies slipped off their chrysalides and in a silky gesture divulged their silky wings. Again and again, a rook flew by low to the ground, batting about like heavy draperies. In another land, far very far away, Heraclius was being anointed emperor of Rome. To the east, Khusru, the king of Persia, was setting his troops on Antioch. And there, past the West and past the unknown ocean, coppery peasants were raising pyramids in the manner of Pharaohs. And from everywhere on earth came human dreams. Each one different, and each one battling against all others, and all of them joined in a desire to survive. And powerful as it was, that desire was driven by an even greater searching need for the origins of life, a relentless quest for another past.

The walking man quickened his pace. Though having meditated on them so long, so often, and so deeply, still he let the dreams go now; with each step they fell from him like dead branches of thought. For, if the history of a land or a people changed its content, did that not also mean that it had changed its meaning? As he reached the city walls, two night watchmen who had been seated back to back in a corner stood up as one and walked toward him fingering their javelins. Recognizing him, they bowed and opened up one side of the double portal. He nodded in acknowledgment. Without looking behind him, he stepped across the threshold of the city and onto the threshold of the desert. Into the glacial air. The breath from his mouth and nostrils drifted away in whitish wafts. The shadow lengthened before him, darker and more intense.

A sudden bewildered whinny rose behind him together with the night watchmen's joyous calls of "Qays! Qays!" Granting them neither word nor glance, Qays reached the portal and stepped across it in turn. He pushed a reticent horse before him. Taking its great neck in his arms, he kissed its forehead and said:

"Go, brother! Go where you please!"

But as the creature only pawed the ground on which it stood, Qays, the poet, bent down for a stone, which he hurled at it with all his strength:

"Go! Go, find your freedom."

After this, he turned toward the city and entered it sobbing. A wild-eyed gallop could be heard dying in the distance.

Khadija stirred in her sleep. She was cold. With the mechanical gesture of a blind woman, she pulled the blankets to her chin. But she felt colder and colder. As if abandoned. Had he left? left forever? She felt the cold sting of storming sand within her. She was swept by the relentless feeling of a happiness lived from beginning to end. For fifteen years, day in and day out, as she looked back through time, there had been happiness, and now, if she were to look before her she would see the place where the path dropped off. The storm swelled into a tempest and she saw herself in the middle of it; soon, she would be a widow, widowed for the third time. She started to run backwards, as fast as she could, toward the first day. A man entered her house, a timid man, average in height. His presence alone had unsettled her.

85

Muhammad entered the desert. And do you know what the desert is? And who will ever tell you what the desert is? Have you heard the desert singing?

It is innumerable sand, scorched white by the daily furnace of the sun and again by the severe cold flash of night. It is improbable dust that lifts as high as the highest peaks then hangs hesitating between earth and the unknown sky. It is hard drops of light that fall from stars to reappear as drops of dew. It is frosty dew and frozen stone. And palm tree roots that siphon the liquid soul of the earth. And the earth breathing slowly like a nursing woman. And coursing sap travelling from pore to pore on tree trunks stiffened by age-old drought. And the fresh and blessed breath of ancient winds. And caravans, horsemen who journey across life and the Arabian Peninsula, leaving behind them echoing, murmuring tracks: joy, grief, hope. Living beings who have yet to be born. Spirits of the dead. Demons with demoniacal longings to become, become men again. Beasts of burden, so laden with wisdom and experience that they're unable to utter a word. Night birds who ruffle their feathers and tuck their heads beneath their left wings. Nocturnal creatures incessantly surveying a nocturnal landscape. And poets who disappeared. Their long memory endures in the memories of others, their words are passed from mouth to ear, from expectation to pleasure. And silence—the silence of the desert that is filled with everything that has ever lived. Animal or vegetal or human. And fire and water. And light and dark. And past and present. And language, desire, and air, each particle emitting its infinitesimal note and its infinitesimal sign in the supreme call of life to life. Have you heard the desert singing?

When he reached the cave, Muhammad stopped by the stunted olive tree. The shadow left his side and he was left alone with himself. The thoughts were also leaving him, reluctantly, hesitatingly. And he was left standing, wavering at the entrance to the cave.

"Enter. Enter peaceful and appeased. Come close. Nearer. Closer. The hour has come!"

No one spoke. No one made the slightest sound. Muhammad entered the cave. He took a few steps and stopped; he was facing the eastern wall and the burrow, large enough for a man, that cleaved it. All things were concrete, even his senses—his overabounding senses. Patches of sand sprinkled the stony ground on which he stood. The small fissure that had formed on the eve intertwined its letters between his feet: *Ya Sin*. He couldn't see the letters. Not yet.

Khadija woke up. She was bathed in sweat. She obliviously reached to her left, feeling for the place where her gentle husband usually slept. She bolted from the bed, threw open the trunk where her clothing was kept, pulled on the first dress that came to hand—a splendid dress—and ran out calling for Bilal in a loud voice. Bilal was already on his way, racing like a white veil in the night.

"The hour has come. Prostrate yourself and listen."

Who spoke? Nothing and no one. The immense stillness was all. Muhammad fell to his knees and curled up like a fetus with his forehead to the ground, fast by the intertwining letters, embryonic in the rock, *Ya Sin*. He closed his eyes, listened. He distinctly heard the boiling breath of water. And he remembered, past all his recollections, he remembered the first memory.

The waters are hot and loving. Their darkness is luminescent. He feels well there; eternity has yet to begin and it has neither duration nor end. Night after night, a voice of flesh sweetly speaks to him in a language that is very simple and very complete, a language without consonants or vowels, a language slow and full as blood dripping drop by drop. And . . . a harsh voice breaks in upon him:

"The hour has come!"

What hour? Come for what? To leave this blessed Paradise?

"The hour has come!"

He turns and stands up blindly, groping. His entire body is gripped by pain, incomprehension, disarray—and the sweet voice sings a song of freedom. He weeps in the flowing waters. Someone coaxes him to take a first step, points out the path that leads to the light of day, urging him to crawl. Again and again! Warning him never to look back, under any circumstances, lest he perish from thirst in the arid underground. He emerges head first, his fists clenched as though he were pulling the world behind him. The pelvic bones settle back into place and the birth sack closes its door on his heels. It felt as though he had just died.

Forty years later, in a cave, a man died to himself. The wings of the past closed behind him like the last page of a familiar book that will never be read again. Somewhere, another Book had opened between the shadows and flickering light of reality. Pens had been set aside and the ink had dried since astral times. And it was said that the Book's last word was written even before the first was given expression in any of the languages of humankind. Someone was turning the pages, moving from the last to the first, from "he" to "I," and the first word was written:

"Read."

The word achieved the power of speech as soon as it was uttered. He said—in a voice so peaceful that it was terrifying, he said:

"Read."

Revelation had come surging from the rock, and it was simple and pure beyond sense and reason. And Muhammad was at one with its coming, and then and there he gathered together all his old and forthcoming doubt and collected his disbelief like so many stones for the raising of an enduring wall that would stand between the earthbound man he had been since birth and the Man of the Book he was being summoned to become in a bat of an instant. Fear was in him, whistling and piercing his lungs with every breath. He knew it to be here now, that which had been on its way since the first dawn; the Event had come, and it had come to him. And with that knowledge came the knowledge that from here on he would be responsible for the lives of others. He was the Messenger. He also knew beyond the shadow of a doubt that new worlds exacted ruins and wars and tears, and that it really took so little for human weakness, beginning with his own, to transform itself one day into triumphant force. And his pain was immense, when he said:

"I cannot read."

Bilal and Khadija ran with winded breath beneath a flat sky dull as earth. Deep in the distance, beyond the fortress of reason and beyond the earliest hint of an undecided dawn, they heard the unspeakable lament:

"I cannot read . . . I cannot read . . . I cannot read . . ."

And then . . . they saw the man they had known and loved for so long emerge from the cave and they no longer recognized him. Neither by what they saw nor by what they heard. He stumbled out, tense as a bow stretched to the breaking point, and he called out to the four horizons in a voice in which the rock, the sky, the trees, the rivers and the sea, the living and the dead were all gathered:

"Read! Read in the name of your Lord who made Creation, who created man from the atom . . ."

He stopped for a moment and bent his head to the side as though to consult someone only he could see or hear, and with all the musics of the world he said:

"Praise God, Lord of all the worlds,
Matrix and Maternal Womb,
Master of the Day of Judgment!
It is You whom we worship
And it is . . ."

He fell convulsing and sobbing onto the naked earth. He clung to it, and kissed it. And it was from there, from the quick of the nourishing mother, that his voice rose again:

"And it is You for whom we listen.
Guide us along the straight path . . ."

"Islam will again become the stranger
it was at the outset."

—*The Prophet Muhammad*

About the Book and Author

It is the 26th day of Ramadan in the year 610, and a handsome man named Muhammad is meditating in a cave on Mount Hira. Fear grips him as he tries to sort out the visions and voices washing over him; and terrified that he is possessed, he leaves the cave to return to Mecca. The day that will transform Muhammad's life—and change the world—has begun.

That day becomes a fluid intermingling of the ordinary and a dreamlike conviction that something indescribable is about to happen. Finally, his disquiet increasing, invading his sleep and forcing him to leave his wife's side, Muhammad returns to the cave on Mount Hira to give birth to the momentous revelations within him.

This finely crafted, poetic novel captures the mystery of religious revelation as it unfolds in all its intensity, providing a unique window on Islam's Prophet. Winner of Morocco's prestigious Grand Prix Atlas in 1996, it was first published in French in 1995 as *L'Homme du Livre*.

Born in Morocco in 1926, DRISS CHRAÏBI embraced French education and culture early on and supported French colonial rule; but he soon became equally critical of the Occidental and Islamic worlds, and his writing often focuses on the unresolved conflicts between the two. Chraïbi practiced medicine for a few years, then turned to writing in 1952. He has published more than a dozen highly acclaimed novels.